Lollipops
and
Latin Roots

BOOK 2

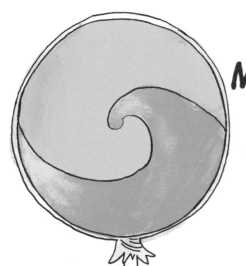

Marilyn Harkrider

ILLUSTRATED BY:
Jerry Vineyard

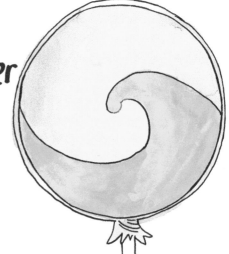

CLAY BRIDGES
PRESS

Lollipops and Latin Roots
Book 2
Wonderful World of Words Series

Copyright © 2018 by Marilyn Harkrider

Published by Clay Bridges in Houston, TX
www.ClayBridgesPress.com

ISBN-10: 1-939815-49-5
ISBN-13: 978-1-939815-49-1
eISBN-10: 1-939815-47-9
eISBN-13: 978-1-939815-47-7

Special Sales: Most Clay Bridges titles are available in special quantity discounts. Custom imprinting or excerpting can also be done to fit special needs. Contact Clay Bridges at Info@ClayBridgesPress.com.

TABLE OF CONTENTS

INTRODUCTION

English did not just happen. It was born out of many people coming together and sharing their words. It changed and grew just like you, and it is still growing and changing just like you are. There are family trees for English words just as you have parents, grandparents, and even great-grandparents. A big word describes this—*etymology*. The more you know about how some words are made, the more you can figure out other words. Have fun exploring your language. It is part of you, and to discover what you are made of is great fun.

A VERY SHORT HISTORY OF ENGLISH

English is a rich and amazing "mutt" language. Many years ago, the Anglo Saxons invaded what is now England. The invaders pushed the Celts, the people who were living there, into what is now called Wales, Scotland, and Ireland. The Celtic languages had little effect on the new language to come. Many of our everyday words, or stock words, come from Anglish brought by the invaders.

Through the Norman invasion from Normandy, France, we gained words and expressions that traveled with their speakers. Many words of government and war came from William the Conqueror of Normandy, France. When he came, the people of the courts spoke French, and the commoners spoke a form of Old English. Anglish, later called English, won the war of words, but many words with French origins remained.

Words of religion and faith from the Catholic Church continued the process of developing our language. The Latin of the church coupled with the French of the Normans brought many Latin roots to our language. On the family tree of languages, both of these languages are on the branch of Romance languages.

Of course, through the years, many other languages have left their marks on English as they brought their rich vocabularies, but the building blocks of the Latin and Greek roots of many of our words give us clues to meanings before we ever need to go to a dictionary. But if you do look at a good dictionary, once you have found the meaning of the word, become a detective and find out where we got that word in the first place. The birth certificate of a word is in the etymological section of its definition.

ETYMO means root, and **LOG** means to study.
Where words come from can be very funny!
Have fun, word detectives. Find the roots
all over the place.

Words mean something. They really do.
And parts of words mean something, too.
The parts you learn you will hear and know.
These parts were created long ago.
Language travels and changes through time.
It was someone else's, now yours and mine.
There are more to explore than the words on these pages.
Learn them all, and you will all be sages.
Sometimes roots come in words, not just one.
Sometimes two roots will double the fun.
Find roots in other words, and you will find
The meaning of those words may come to mind.

(Spanish words that have similar roots are found under the
English word in this book. Sometimes, words from different
languages are very much alike.)

A SIMPLE SPANISH PRONUNCIATION KEY FOR STARTERS

Some sounds take practice before you can sound like a native speaker, but this guide will help you start. Spanish has fewer sounds for its letters than English. It does have a few more letters in its alphabet.

Vowels have only one sound.

A – ah		**I** – ee		**U** – oo	
E – eh		**O** – oh			

Consonants generally sound the same as in English. Here are the main exceptions.

C – Before *E* or *I*, it sounds like an *S* as in "sink" (in Spain, *th*). Before *A*, *O*, or *U*, it sounds like a *K* as in "cube."

CH – Sounds like the *CH* in "check."

G – Before *E* or *I*, it sounds like an *H* as in "happy." Before *A*, *O*, or *U*, it sounds like a *G* as in "go."

H - It has no sound.

J - Its sound is like an *H* in English.

LL – Sounds like a *Y*.

Ñ – Sounds like the *N* in "ca(ny)on."

RR - Takes practice and the trilling of the tongue. Right now, while you practice, use an *R* sound.

X – Sounds like *KS* as in "socks," or (mostly names) as a raspy *H*.

Z – Sounds like an *S* or, in parts of Spain, *th.*

Remember, Spanish has many accents just like English. British English does not sound like American English, and the Spanish spoken in Spain does not sound exactly like the Spanish spoken in the "New World." (Spain brought Spanish to Central and South America.)

If you want to learn to speak like a native speaker, there are many sites on the Internet.

HAVE FUN PRACTICING IN A MEXICAN RESTAURANT.

ROOT WORDS TO LEARN

accelerate

AC means toward, and **CELER** means quick.

If done way too fast, you might become sick.

accelerate

acelerar

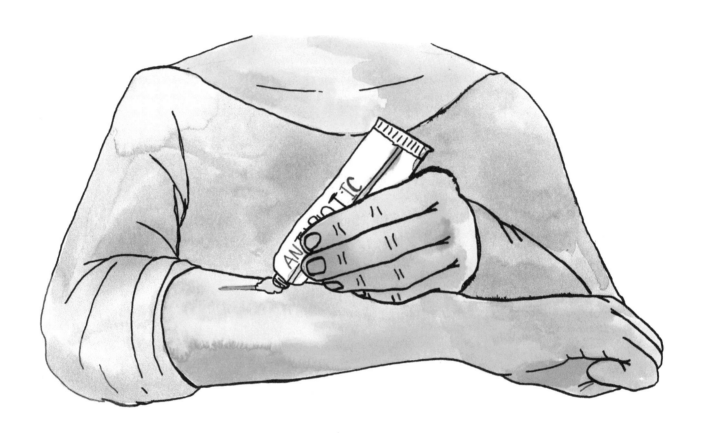

antibiotic

ANTI is against, and **BIO** means life.

Put this on, please, if you are cut with a knife.

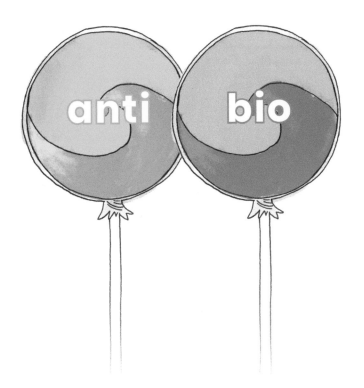

antibiotic

antibiótico

astrology

LOGY means study, and **ASTRO** means star.

In this class, you need the telescope to see far.

astrology

astrología

astronaut

ASTRO means star, and **NAUT** means a ship.

They fly to the stars. What an incredible trip!

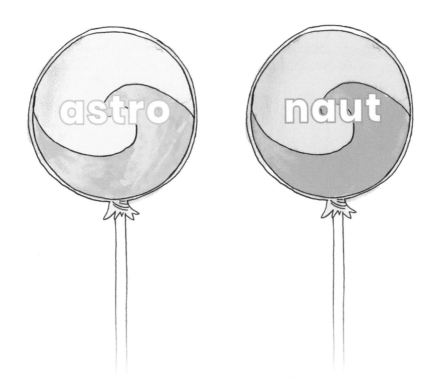

astronaut

astronauto

audiovisual

AUD is to hear, and **VIS** is to see.

You experience this when at a movie.

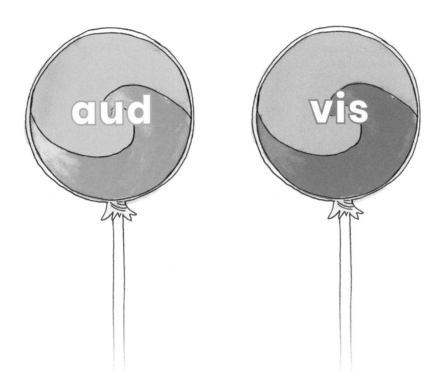

audio **vis**ual

audiovisual

automobile

AUTO means self, and **MOB** means to move.

If you drive this correctly, all will approve.

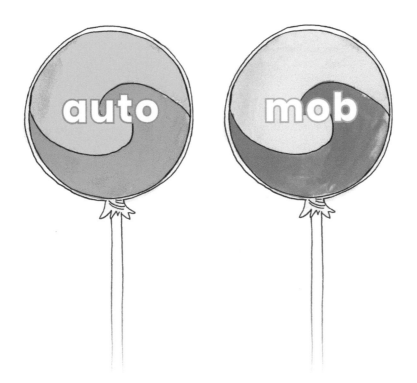

automobile

automóvil

bicycle

BI means two Greek though it be,

CYCL means circle, so ride . . . Watch the tree!!

bicycle

bicicleta

biography

BIO means life, and **GRAPH** means record.

A book of this kind might have a man with a sword.

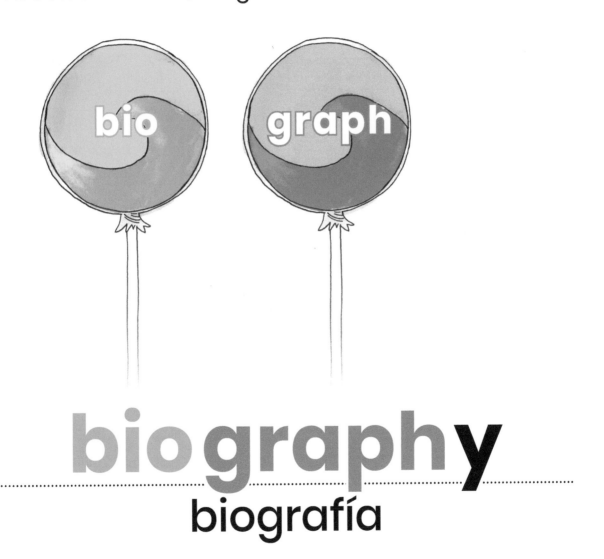

bio graphy

biografía

biology

BIO means life, and **LOGY** means study.

So when you're in this class, you might have a froggy.

biology
biología

carnivore

VOR is to eat, and **CARNI** means meat.

You can pick up fried chicken, but please be discreet.

carnivore

carnívoro

conduct

CON means with, and **DUCT** means to lead.

In music, you may use what looks like a reed.

con **duct**

----

conducir

contradict

CONTRA means against, and **DIC** means to speak.

If you do this, be nice and don't make people freak.

contra dict

contradecir

(**decir** means "to say" in Spanish)

decelerate

CELER means quick, and DE means reduce,

Doing this action, your speed you will lose.

de celer ate

decelerar

democracy

DEMO means people, and **CRACY** is power.

So we rule, not others. The government's ours.

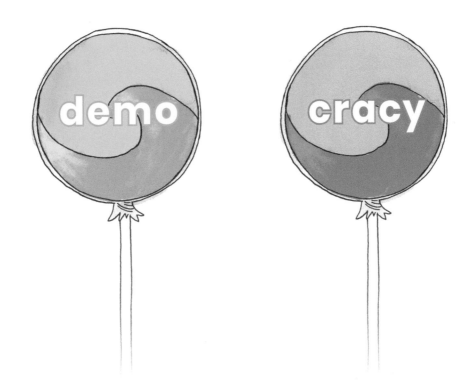

democracy

democracia

eject

E means out, and **JECT** is to throw.

Push the button in an airplane, out the pilot will go.

eject

expulsar

(related to the English word "expulsion")

extraterrestrial

EXTRA is beyond, and **TERR** means earth.

What they may look like can cause us great mirth.

extraterrestrial

extraterrestre

geography

GEO means earth, and **GRAPH** means record in Greek.

So this is a study of mountains and creeks.

geo graph

geography
geografía

herbivore

HERBI means plant, and **VOR** means to eat.

Eating your vegetables should be a treat.

herbivore

herbívoro

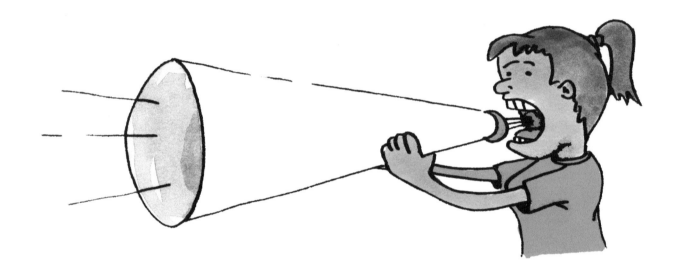

megaphone

MEGA means large, and sound for **PHON**,

That makes your voice louder, so watch your tone.

megaphone

megáfono

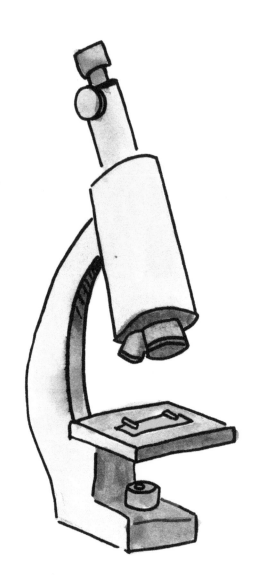

microscope

MICRO means small, and **SCOPE** means to see.

Use this to look at things that are wee.

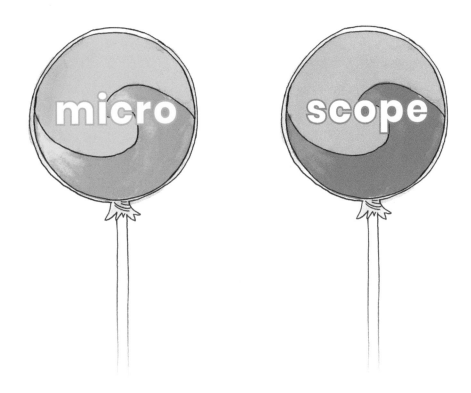

microscope

microscopio

odometer

OD means path, and **METER** to measure,

The distance of fun travels. Oh what a pleasure!

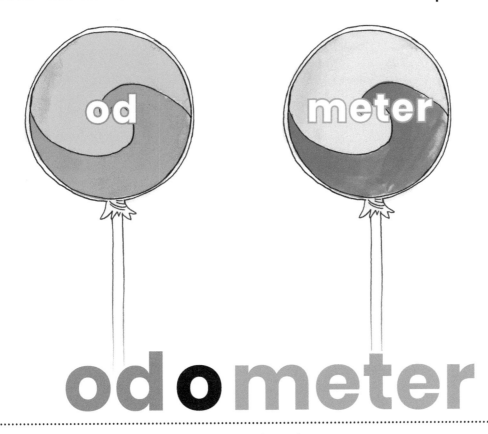

odometer

cuentakilómetros

(Cuenta means count. Kilometers are used in many countries instead of miles.)

proclaim

PRO means before, and **CLAM** means speak out.

But in front of a crowd, you don't have to shout.

pro clai m

proclamar

recline

RE is back, **CLINE** is lean; those are facts,

So get in that chair; push it back and relax.

re cline

reclinar

submarine

MAR means sea, and **SUB** means under.

A submarine goes down beneath the water.

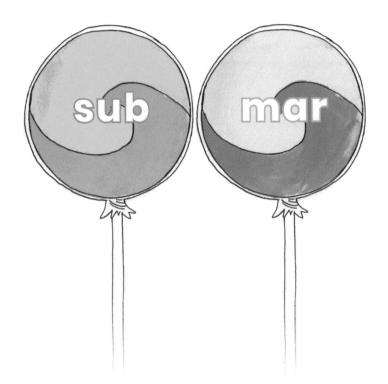

sub mar ine
submarine

telephone

TELE means far, and **PHON** means sound.

You can talk to your friends when they're not around.

telephone

teléfono

telescope

TELE means far and **SCOPE** means to see.

You can see stars though faraway they may be.

tele scope

telescopio

transport

TRANS means across, and **PORT** means to carry.

Airplanes do this, and so does a ferry.

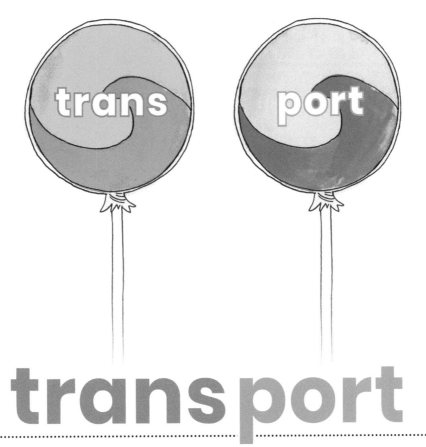

transport

transporte

(v. transporter)

LOLLIPOPS FOR THE CLASSROOM AND HOME

I would love for you to use these lollipops in your classroom or home to help your children and students learn their roots. Feel free to copy them, enlarge them, color them, glue them on popsicle sticks or whatever you like to make the learning experience more fun! You can even use them in the games listed in the "Lollipop Games" section of this book.

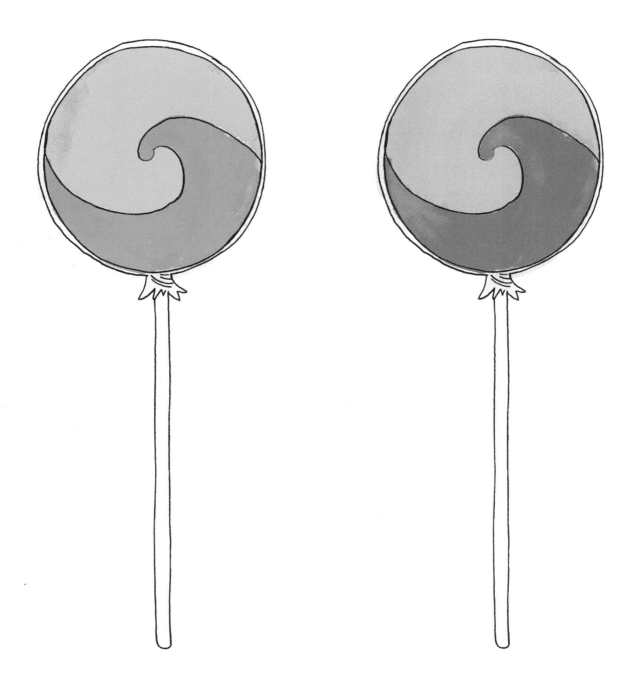

LOLLIPOP GAMES

LOLLIPOP GARDENS

LOLLIPOP GARDEN 1 (classroom/home)

1. Use the prototype and popsicle sticks to create a lollipop for each root.

2. As a child masters the root, "plant" the lollipop in the "garden."

LOLLIPOP GARDEN 2 (classroom/home)

1. Use the prototype and popsicle sticks to create a lollipop for each root. Print the root on the prototype and stick the popsicle stick in the "garden."

2. Make petals that can be glued to the circle.

3. As new words using the root are found, print them on the "petals."

4. Attach each petal to the circle to create a flower.

LOLLIPOP GARDEN 3 (classroom)

1. Use the prototype and popsicle sticks to create a lollipop for each root. Print the root on the prototype and stick the popsicle stick in the "garden."

2. Make petals that can be glued to the circle.

3. As students meet the criteria you set up for the class, print their names on a petal.

4. Attach the petals to the circle to create a flower.

LOLLIPOP TREE (classroom/home)

1. Make a lollipop with the prototype and a small dowel rod or popsicle stick.

2. Print the root on the circle.

3. Purchase a large styrofoam cone, or use a small branch.

4. As a child learns the root, put it on the tree.

Note: The gardens and the tree remind the children of their successes and keep the root before them on a day-to-day basis.

LOLLIPOP BORDER (classroom/home)

1. Use the prototype and popsicle sticks to create colorful lollipops with the roots written on them.

2. Make a border to decorate the child's room or the classroom.

3. Using the border, play the game "I Spy." "I spy with my little eye a root that means . . ."

LOLLIPOP MATCHING (classroom/home)

1. Using the prototype and popsicle sticks, make pairs of lollipops, one with a root and one with the meaning or word containing that root.

2. Put the pairs face down on a table or on the floor.

3. Have players take turns turning over lollipops for matches.

4. When a match is made, the player takes the two lollipops and continues until no match is made.

5. The winner is the player with the most lollipops.

HIDE THE LOLLIPOP (classroom/home)

This game can be done in one day or over several days.

1. Using the prototype and popsicle sticks, make lollipops with either the meaning or the root on a lollipop.

2. Hide the lollipops for the children to find.

3. When a lollipop is found, the child must give the meaning or root in order to claim the lollipop.

4. If the child gives the answer, the lollipop is put into the "licked" pile, not to be rehidden.

5. When all lollipops are found, the child gets a prize.

(If a lollipop is hidden and found each day, a lollipop can be given for a correct answer.)

LOLLIPOP POP UP (classroom)

1. Using the prototype and popsicle sticks, make lollipops with the roots printed on the circles.

2. Make enough sets for several teams.

3. When the teams are selected, give each team a set of lollipops.

4. Give the meaning of one of the roots on a lollipop.

5. The first team to hold up the root meaning gets the point.

6. Play until all the meanings are given or one team gets a certain number of points.

LOLLIPOP RELAY (classroom)

1. Using the prototype and popsicle sticks, make lollipops with the roots printed on the circles.

2. Put the lollipops on the wall or a bulletin board within reach of the children.

3. Divide the children into teams.

4. Read the meaning of a root.

5. The first team to claim the root gets it.

The team with the most lollipops at the end of the game wins.

Note: With an overhead projector, project the roots on the wall, and the children can "slap" the correct root. You can keep score on paper.

POP A LOLLIPOP (classroom/home)

1. Each child makes a set of lollipops with the roots written on the circle. (Any number may be used for the game.)

2. The children place the roots that are to be used that day on their desks or a table.

3. The teacher or parent gives the meaning of one of the roots. The children hold up the root they think is correct. Each child with the correct root gets a point.

4. A meaning can be given more than once to allow a second chance for those who may not have gotten the root correctly the first time. That encourages children to pay attention to learn for the next time.

5. Points for the day or week can be charted, if desired, or prizes for a certain number of points can be awarded, if desired.

Note: For ease in counting the number of correct responses, have half the class play the game while the other half is involved in a quiet seat activity, if possible.

LOLLI LAND (classroom/home)

1. Lolli Land is played like Candy Land but with roots written on the colored lollipops. (Special lollipop spaces with no roots on the board can have pictures drawn from the stack of cards to either advance or go back.)

2. When a student lands on a lollipop root, he or she must give the meaning correctly or lose a turn. (Have a list of the root meanings for reference, if needed, to settle questions.)

3. The first to get to Lolli Land wins.

Note: The board made with lollipops is fun and special, but the regular game of Candy Land can be used and adapted.

LOLLIPOP LEAP (classroom/home)

1. Make a regular hopscotch board with chalk, but instead of using squares, use circles with sticks to make lollipops.
2. Write Latin roots in the circles.
3. Have the children jump the roots, giving meanings as they go.
4. If a child misses a root meaning, he or she can start over later and learn from others who are jumping.

Note: Physical activity helps cement learning.

LOLLIPOP UP (classroom)

1. Make lollipops with the roots or meanings on them (one set per student). (This is a good learning tool if the children made their own sets.)
2. Call out a meaning or root.
3. The children who "pop up" first with the correct answer get a point. (It can be either the first to "pop up" or on a specific

count, allowing for more "winners." If they give the incorrect answer, they lose a point.

This can be done game-by-game or with a running score, allowing children to study to get more correct answers.

Children can be at their desks or sitting on the floor.

LOLLI LOGIC

It is logical that the roots you learned are used in other places.

1. Divide the children into teams (individuals can do it, but groups might be more fun).

2. Give a root or several to the groups.

3. After a certain amount of time, have the groups find new words using the root(s). They may use a dictionary or any other source allowed. Meanings must accompany the word. (Variation: The first team that gets a new word with the meaning gets a point.)

    Note: Computers may take the fun out of this since they would probably have ready-made lists. Spelling counts. If a word is misspelled, it does not count.

4. Have the groups post their findings in the classroom.

5. The team with the most points wins.

CPSIA information can be obtained
at www.ICGtesting.com
Printed in the USA
LVHW07s1938100918
589679LV00015B/91/P